Dear Parents and Educators,

Welcome to Penguin Young Readers! As parents and educators, you know that each child develops at his or her own pace—in terms of speech, critical thinking, and, of course, reading. Penguin Young Readers recognizes this fact. As a result, each Penguin Young Readers book is assigned a traditional easy-to-read level (1–4) as well as a Guided Reading Level (A–P). Both of these systems will help you choose the right book for your child. Please refer to the back of each book for specific leveling information. Penguin Young Readers features esteemed authors and illustrators, stories about favorite characters, fascinating nonfiction, and more!

A Pig, a Fox, and Stinky Socks

LEVEL 2

GUIDED READING LEVEL I

This book is perfect for a **Progressing Reader** who:

- can figure out unknown words by using picture and context clues;
- can recognize beginning, middle, and ending sounds;
- can make and confirm predictions about what will happen in the text; and
- can distinguish between fiction and nonfiction.

Here are some **activities** you can do during and after reading this book:

- Rhyming Words: On a separate piece of paper, make a list of all the rhyming words in this story. For example, *pail* rhymes with *mail*, so write those two words next to each other.
- Compare/Contrast: In this book, we find out that Fox is little and Pig is big. In what other ways are they different? What do they have in common?

Remember, sharing the love of reading with a child is the best gift you can give!

—Sarah Fabiny, Editorial Director
Penguin Young Readers program

*Penguin Young Readers are leveled by independent reviewers applying the standards developed by Irene Fountas and Gay Su Pinnell in *Matching Books to Readers: Using Leveled Books in Guided Reading*, Heinemann, 1999.

For Mima, Papa, Grandma, and Grandpa—JF

PENGUIN YOUNG READERS
An Imprint of Penguin Random House LLC

 Published by Penguin Young Readers, an imprint of Penguin Random House LLC, 345 Hudson Street, New York, New York 10014. Manufactured in China.

Library of Congress Cataloging-in-Publication Data is available.

ISBN 9780515157802 (pbk) 10 9 8 7 6 5 4 3 2
ISBN 9780515157819 (hc) 10 9 8 7 6 5 4 3 2 1

PENGUIN YOUNG READERS

LEVEL 2 PROGRESSING READER

A PIG, A FOX, AND STINKY SOCKS

by Jonathan Fenske

Penguin Young Readers
An Imprint of Penguin Random House

PART ONE

I am little.
I am big.
HOP
HOP
HOP

I have some socks.
I like to play.
I think I will trick
Pig today.

This pair of socks
was on my feet.

This pair of socks does
NOT smell sweet.

I have a pretty little box.

I fill it with the stinky socks.
To: Pig
From: Fox

And hide inside
this handy pail.
LAUNDRY

To watch Pig find
his stinky mail.
LAUNDRY

A little box!
What can this be?
Hee
Hee!
LAUNDRY
To: Pig
From: Fox
Oh, can it be
a gift for me?
To: Pig
From: Fox

What is inside?
I cannot tell.
SHAKE
SHAKE
I lift the lid.
What is that smell?

The only thing inside this box is one old pair of stinky socks.

These socks do not go in my MAIL.
They go inside my LAUNDRY PAIL.
LAUNDRY

Uh-oh.
LAUNDRY

Now who would give me smelly socks?

That really stinks.

And so does Fox.
LAUNDRY

PART TWO

He is Fox.
He is Pig.
Yuck.

He is little.
He is big.

Oh, I am such a sneaky Fox!
I have ANOTHER pair of socks.

Another pair of socks that stink.
Another funny trick I think.

I have Pig's bowl.
I have Pig's slop.
SLOP
Socks on bottom.
Slop on top.
SLOP

I put Pig's favorite spoon inside.
Now I must find a place to hide.
GARBAGE

Here comes Pig!
I must be quick!
This empty can
should do the
trick.
GARBAGE

A bowl of slop!
Oh, what a treat!
Hee
Hee!
GARBAGE
Yum! Yum! I cannot
wait to eat!

But wait! What is inside my slop?
That sneaky Fox. He has to stop.

That sneaky Fox.
He is so bad!
That sneaky Fox.
He makes me mad!

I would not EVER want to eat the socks from Fox's stinky feet!

My slop was ruined by those socks.
GARBAGE
That really stinks.
GA AGE

And so does Fox.
GA AGE

PART THREE

I am Fox.
I am Pig.

I am little.
I am big.

I had my fun.
I had my laugh.